Puff, the Magic Dragon

From the library of:

_____

_____

Puff, the Magic Dragon

PETER YARROW

LENNY LIPTON

with paintings by

ERIC PUYBARET

STERLING

New York / London

PUFF, THE MAGIC DRAGON, lived by the sea,

And frolicked in the autumn mist in a land called Honalee.

Little Jackie Paper loved that rascal Puff,
And brought him strings and sealing wax and other fancy stuff.

Puff, the magic dragon, lived by the sea,

And frolicked in the autumn mist in a land called Honalee.

Puff, the magic dragon, lived by the sea,

And frolicked in the autumn mist in a land called Honalee.

Together they would travel on a boat with billowed sail.
Jackie kept a lookout perched on Puff's gigantic tail.

Noble kings and princes would bow whene'er they came.

Pirate ships would lower their flag when Puff roared out his name.

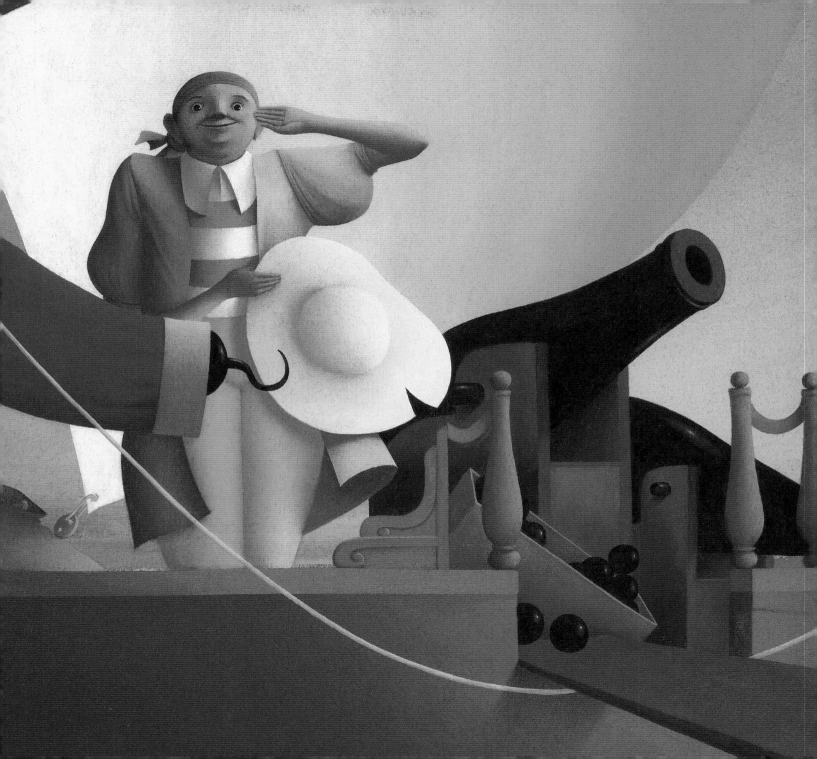

Puff, the magic dragon, lived by the sea,
And frolicked in the autumn mist in a land called Honalee.

Puff, the magic dragon, lived by the sea,
And frolicked in the autumn mist in a land called Honalee.

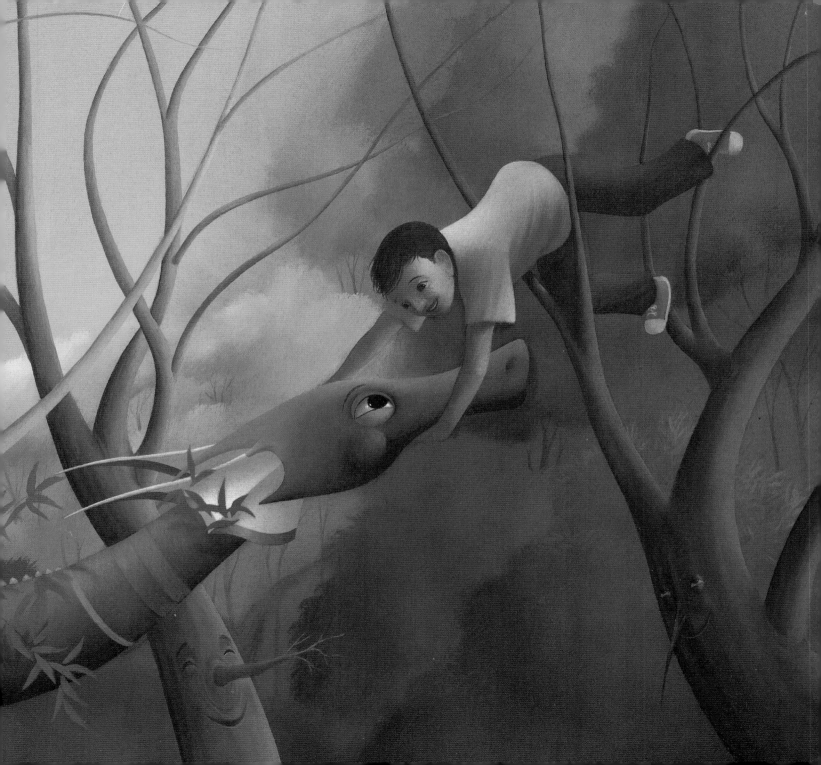

A dragon lives forever, but not so little girls and boys.
Painted wings and giants' rings make way for other toys.

One gray night it happened, Jackie Paper came no more,
And Puff, that mighty dragon, he ceased his fearless roar.

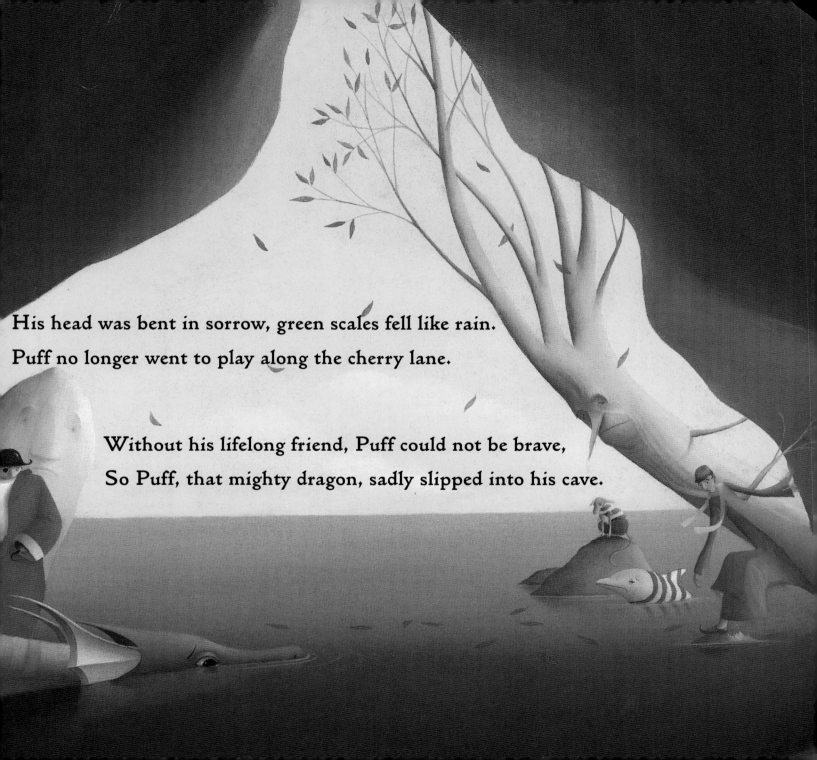

His head was bent in sorrow, green scales fell like rain.
Puff no longer went to play along the cherry lane.

Without his lifelong friend, Puff could not be brave,
So Puff, that mighty dragon, sadly slipped into his cave.

Puff, the magic dragon, lived by the sea,
And frolicked in the autumn mist in a land called Honalee.

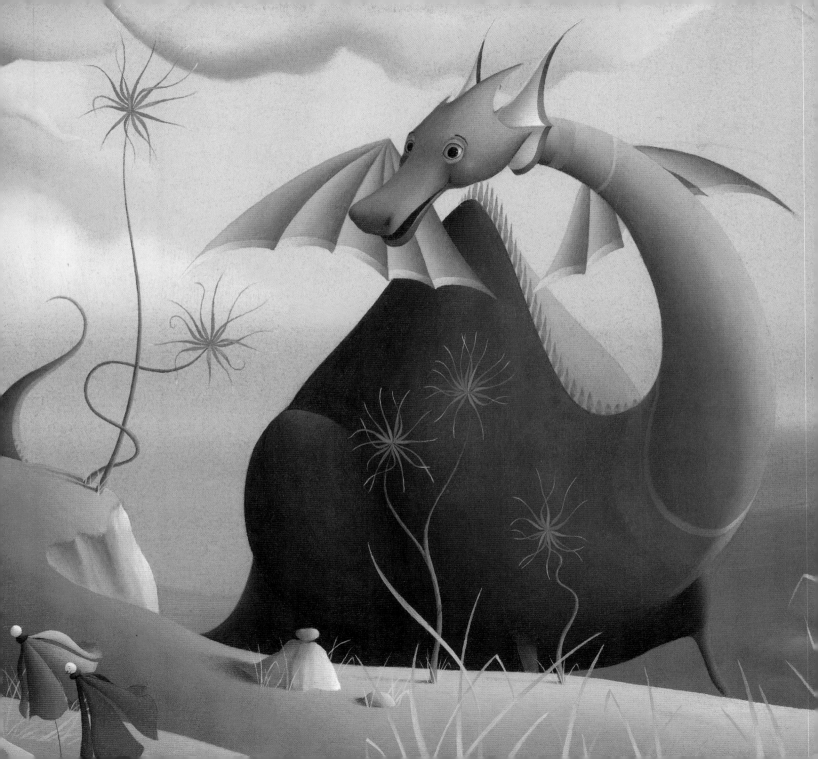

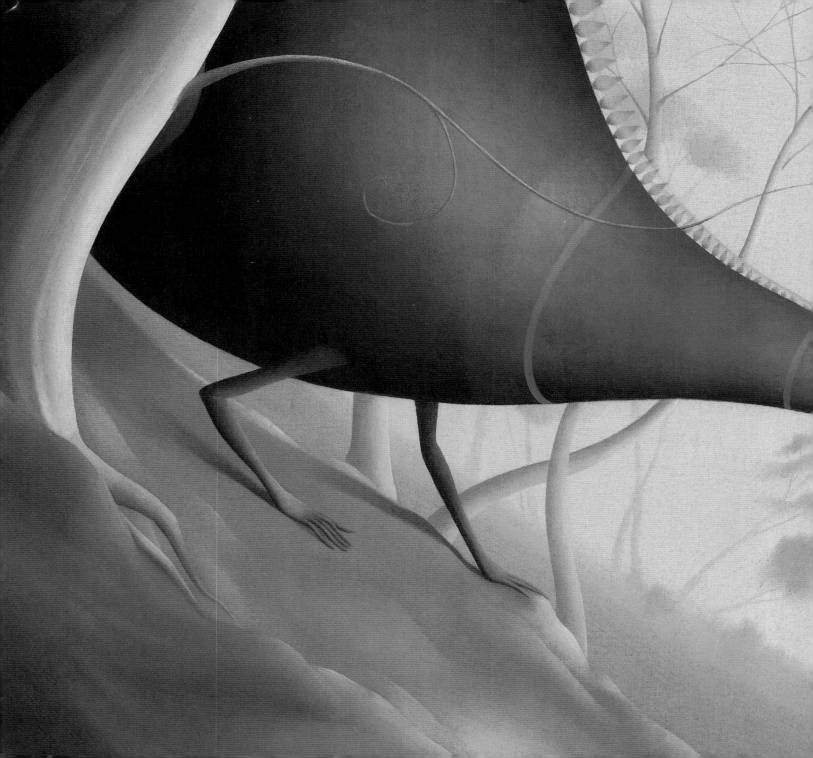

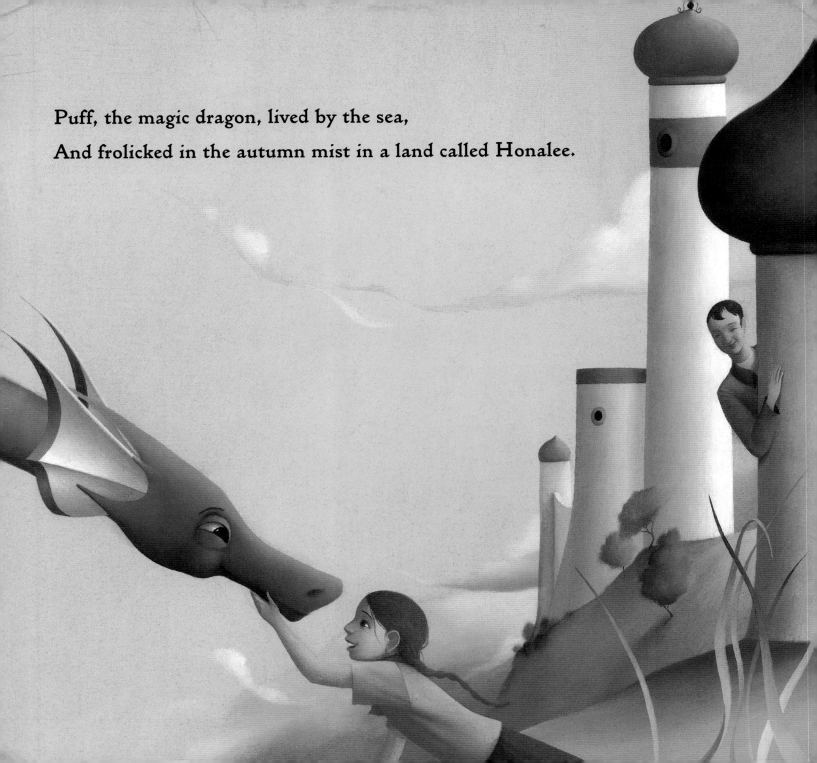

Puff, the magic dragon, lived by the sea,
And frolicked in the autumn mist in a land called Honalee.

FROM THE AUTHORS

OVER THE YEARS, *Puff, the Magic Dragon* has changed a lot for me because of the thousands of stories people have told me and my singing partners after our Peter, Paul & Mary concerts. They've shared how the song moved them as children, how it made them cry, and how they've sung it to their own children and grandchildren.

Puff has appeared to me both childlike and wise, a king but also a willing follower of just about any bright spirit that inspired him. Puff gives his whole heart and soul to one special friend, Jackie Paper. And though it is terribly painful when Jackie grows up and has to leave, Puff has given Jackie the strength and courage he needs to believe in himself when he goes back to the real world. One day, as you can see at the end of this book, a new and special friend comes to Honalee to play with Puff. In this way, Puff and Jackie's friendship continues through new children like you.

I love the spirit of Honalee's gentleness, which offers rest and peace to all who come to know it. You can feel that spirit in this book's beautiful illustrations and you can also hear it in the very special version of *Puff* that I recorded with my daughter, Bethany. I'm so pleased for you to meet her, just as Puff will be very pleased to meet you as you wander through his new, amazing book.

Peter Yarrow

I WAS ONCE ON the island of Kauai with my family and friends and we came across a gigantic lava cave on the edge of Hanalei Bay. My friend asked me how I came to set *Puff, the Magic Dragon* here and I told him the truth: I had never heard of Hanalei and I had no idea it had a cave fit for a dragon. I can't explain it, and like so much of life, this is another mystery to accept and enjoy.

Puff, the Magic Dragon has become part of our culture, and every day of my life I wonder how it was that I came to play a part in its creation. There are many what-ifs along the way to *Puff*. I left a poem in Peter Yarrow's typewriter and he added some new lyrics and turned it into a song. If I had taken what I had written seriously, I would have kept that piece of paper and Peter might never have seen it. And if Peter hadn't met Paul and Mary, it's probable that nobody would have ever heard of Puff.

I think of Puff as a gift, as much for me as for you. So I would like to thank you, the reader, for making Puff what he is today.

Lenny Lipton

STERLING and the distinctive Sterling logo are registered trademarks
of Sterling Publishing Co., Inc.

LIBRARY OF CONGRESS CATALOGING-IN-PUBLICATION DATA AVAILABLE

Published by Sterling Publishing Co., Inc., 387 Park Avenue South, New York, New York 10016
Text © 2007 by Peter Yarrow and Lenny Lipton. Illustrations © 2007 by Eric Puybaret.
Distributed in Canada by Sterling Publishing
c/o Canadian Manda Group, 165 Dufferin Street
Toronto, Ontario, Canada M6K 3H6
Distributed in the United Kingdom by GMC Distribution Services
Castle Place, 166 High Street, Lewes, East Sussex, England BN7 1XU
Distributed in Australia by Capricorn Link (Australia) Pty. Ltd.
P.O. Box 704, Windsor, NSW 2756, Australia

The illustrations in this book were done using acrylic on linen.
The display lettering was created by Judythe Sieck.
The text type was set in ITC Golden.
Designed by Lauren Rille and Scott Piehl

Sterling ISBN 978-1-4027-7216-0

For information about custom editions, special sales, premium and corporate purchases,
please contact Sterling Special Sales Department at 800-805-5489 or
specialsales@sterlingpublishing.com